SAFARI SURVIVAL

J. BURCHETT & S. VOGLER

STONE ARCH BOOKS
a capstone imprint

Wild Rescue books are published by Stone Arch Books
A Capstone Imprint
1710 Roe Crest Drive
North Mankato, Minnesota 56003
www.capstonepub.com

First published by Stripes Publishing Ltd.
1 The Coda Centre
189 Munster Road
London SW6 6AW
© Jan Burchett and Sara Vogler, 2012
Interior art © Diane Le Feyer of Cartoon Saloon, 2012

Cataloging-in-Publication Data is available at the Library of Congress website.

ISBN: 978-1-4342-9057-1

Summary: Ben and Zoe rush to the Kenyan savannah to investigate the rapidly
decreasing African elephant population. The twins soon discover that a group of
hunters has been killing the endangered species for sport — and now they have
their sights set on a mother elephant and her calf! The race is on for Ben and Zoe
to track down the elephants before the hunters do.

Cover Art: Sam Kennedy
Graphic Designer: Russell Griesmer
Production Specialist: Michelle Biedscheid

Design Credits: Shutterstock 51686107 (p. 4-5),
Shutterstock 51614464 (back cover, p. 148-149, 150, 152)

Printed in China by Nordica.
1013/CA21301906
092013
007736NORDS14

TABLE OF CONTENTS

CHAPTER 1: SNARED......................7

CHAPTER 2: OWL........................18

CHAPTER 3: SAMBURU NATIONAL PARK......28

CHAPTER 4: FRANK HALL.................49

CHAPTER 5: LESTER HALL...............54

CHAPTER 6: UNDERCOVER................64

CHAPTER 7: CHITUNDU..................71

CHAPTER 8: ON THE HUNT...............83

CHAPTER 9: PROWLER...................97

CHAPTER 10: TOMBOI...................110

CHAPTER 11: SAFE AND SOUND..........143

MISSION

BEN WOODWARD
WILD Operative

ZOE WOODWARD
WILD Operative

WILD RESCUE

BRIEFING

TARGET:

CODE NAME: TOMBOI

CHAPTER 1

SNARED

"Take cover," Ben whispered to Zoe. "There's someone coming."

His twin sister tried to dive aside, but it was too late. A shadowy figure, face hidden beneath a black mask, stepped out in front of her and held up a rifle.

Zap! Zoe saw a flash on her chest. She was hit. She let out a frustrated sigh.

The stranger whipped off her mask and grinned. "Erika!" said Zoe. "What are you doing at Lasertrail?"

"Trailing you two," Erika said. She grinned again and turned off her laser rifle. "Your uncle sent me. WILD has a new mission for you."

"Cool!" said Ben. "So are we off to WILD HQ for our mission briefing?"

"No time for that," said Erika, guiding them to the exit. "We're going straight to Africa. My car's waiting outside to take us to the airplane. I've already told your grandma about your mission, so she won't be expecting you home today."

Ben and Zoe looked at each other with excitement. Ever since their eccentric uncle, Dr. Stephen Fisher, had recruited them into WILD, they'd found themselves traveling all over the world. Their parents were veterinarians who were currently working abroad.

Their mom and dad thought Ben and Zoe were safe at home, enjoying their summer vacation with their grandmother. But really, the twins were traveling the world saving animals — just like their parents were.

Erika, Ben, and Zoe sped along a deserted country road in Erika's car. "This must be a really urgent mission," said Ben. "What's it all about?"

"You'll find out once we're airborne," Erika said. "You know Dr. Fisher prefers to explain things himself."

A small airstrip soon came into view. Erika drove the car to a waiting private jet. They scrambled aboard, and then Erika began the pre-flight checks.

They soared into the sky and were soon out over the sea.

"So, what's our mission this time, Erika?" Ben asked.

Erika flicked a switch. A shimmering hologram appeared in the air. It was their uncle. He wore his usual straw hat perched atop of his messy hair.

"Greetings, my nephew and niece," he said. "If you press the red button on the console in front of you, you'll find a clue to your mission — and it's a big clue. Contact me when you've figured out which animal it comes from."

And with that, the hologram disappeared. Zoe pressed a button, opening a small compartment. Resting inside was a glass eyeball.

Ben and Zoe studied it. The iris was golden brown with a round black pupil.

"Uncle Stephen said it was a big clue," said Zoe, puzzled, "but this isn't a very big eyeball. I wonder what he meant."

"It has to be an animal from Africa," Ben said, turning the eye over in his hand. "Maybe a lion, or a leopard . . . wait a minute! He meant it's the biggest animal."

Ben flicked a switch next to the speaker that connected to WILD HQ. "Are you there, Uncle Stephen?"

"I hear you loud and clear," said Dr. Fisher. "Have you cracked the puzzle already?"

"It's an elephant," said Ben.

"Well done," said their uncle. "An African elephant, in fact. They're bigger than the Indian ones — and more dangerous." He sounded concerned. "Here at WILD, we've received a message from a charity worker out in Kenya. There's a bull calf called Tomboi in trouble in the Samburu National Park. He has a wire snare wrapped around his leg and it could easily get infected. He and his mother are already starting to trail behind the herd."

"So our job is to find the injured elephant?" asked Zoe.

"Exactly," said Uncle Stephen. "Find him, then sedate the little fella so you can remove the snare. Then I need you to give him some antibiotics. I'm afraid that is his only chance of survival."

"There's a veterinary kit under your seat inside your backpack," Erika said.

Ben grabbed the small backpack and examined the tranquilizer guns and medication bottles inside. "This is the sort of equipment that Mom and Dad use in the field," he said excitedly.

"The tranquilizer guns are not just for Tomboi," Erika told them. "There are dangerous wild animals in Kenya. Have them ready whenever you're out on your own."

Zoe opened her backpack. "Sleeping bag, food rations, binoculars, night-vision goggles, and of course my BUG," she said, taking out the small gizmo that looked like a hand-held videogame console. She tapped a key to bring up a satellite map of their current location.

"Hey! This plane's super fast," Zoe said. "We're already halfway there."

"One thing puzzles me, Uncle Stephen," Ben said. "How did the snare get around Tomboi's leg? He lives on a wildlife reserve. Isn't game hunting illegal in Kenya?"

"It is," said Dr. Fisher's voice. "I'm afraid we've stumbled upon some bad news. Someone is hunting these elephants. People in the local village claim that several elephant carcasses have been found nearby."

"Were the elephants shot?" asked Zoe.

"Yes," her uncle said solemnly. "And then the heads and tusks were taken, as well as their skins. Some were only youngsters."

"Disgusting," Ben said.

"That's horrible," said Zoe.

"Now you know how urgent this case is," said Uncle Stephen. "We believe that Tomboi's injury is linked to the elephant killings. There were signs that at least one of the dead calves had been snared, too."

"Why haven't you told the local authorities?" asked Zoe.

"The Kenya Wildlife Service protects a huge area of land and is very overworked," said their uncle. "It can't investigate every report without solid evidence. And so far, all we have is a few carcasses. And if we told them about Tomboi's leg, they might not be able to get to him right away. With the hunters at large, he's in danger right now — and still would be when he was released back into the wild."

"Although our first priority is to heal his leg, we've decided on a rather risky plan," Erika added. "Once you've treated Tomboi, leave him and his mother there and try to find out who these hunters are."

"And try to get the evidence to put them in prison," their uncle added. "Are you willing to take on this dangerous mission?"

"Try to stop us!" said Ben. Zoe nodded.

Uncle Stephen smiled. "I knew I could count on you two," he said. "Keep me updated." His image disappeared as he cut communication.

CHAPTER 2

OWL

"We have to get to Tomboi before anything else happens to him," said Zoe.

Ben nodded. "And we have to find out who's behind all this," he added.

Erika took out a small case from her pocket and tossed it to Zoe. Inside was a metallic disc about the size of a thumbtack.

"Your uncle has invented these to help you gather information," said Erika.

"What is it?" Zoe asked.

"It's called an OWL device," Erika said. "OWL stands for 'Outstanding Watching and Listening.' It's perfect for tracking animals — or humans. As soon as you press it on a target, it attaches itself with a powerful adhesive. It has a miniature camera and microphone that transmits directly to your BUGs."

"Cool," said Zoe. "And it's so tiny."

"I'll give you a demonstration of how it works," said Erika, tapping some keys. "Turn your BUGs to OWL mode."

Ben and Zoe scrolled through their menus to OWL and hit their ENTER keys.

At once, a high-tech computer program flashed up on their screens.

"That's the Control Room in WILD HQ," Ben said.

"Welcome to the Outstanding Watching and Listening device interface," Uncle Stephen's voice said through their BUGs. "You should be seeing what I'm seeing right now — the Control Room in WILD HQ. It's being transmitted by the OWL attached to my hat! If the image is a little jerky, it's because I'm walking around."

The picture swung around to show the coffee machine. Then it showed Uncle Stephen's desk, which was covered in a jumble of papers, wires, and various tools.

"His desk is as messy as ever!" Ben said to Zoe and Erika. "I wonder what he's inventing now?"

"You're probably wondering what I'm inventing now," said Uncle Stephen. "It's actually an automatic egg cracker, which I've been —"

There was a muffled thump as the scene lurched sideways. The children could see under the desk now. There was a mess of discarded candy wrappers and writing utensils.

Then the image spun to reveal their uncle's face. He'd taken off his hat and was peering into the OWL's camera. His cheeks were red and his hair was standing on end.

"Sorry about that!" he said, smiling but obviously embarrassed. "I tripped over my chair and took a little spill."

Ben grinned at Zoe. Their uncle was a brilliant man, but he was pretty clumsy sometimes.

"Good luck with your mission," said Uncle Stephen as he brushed himself off. "Over and out!" He waited a few moments. Then he grinned. "Well, it will be over and out when you switch off the OWL camera."

Ben and Zoe rolled their eyes and hit their OFF buttons.

"The OWL also sends a signal to the satellite map on your BUG screens," said Erika. "Turn them on and see for yourself."

They did as she said and a world map appeared.

A tiny red light was pulsing over the North Sea. When they zoomed in they saw it was directly on top of WILD's secret island headquarters.

"So it's a tracker, too," Zoe said.

Ben turned to face the onboard computer. He opened the Internet browser. "I'm going to find out everything I can about the Samburu National Park," he said. He read from one page. "It's near the foothills of Mount Kenya. The tribe that lives there is known as the Samburu." Ben scrolled down. "It says here they keep an eye on the elephant herd and take tourists out to see them. So they'll be able to find out where Tomboi is. And we might pick up some info on the slaughtered elephants." He brought up another website and was soon lost in thought while reading the information.

"Interesting!" Ben said. "Elephants can live to age seventy. Females and young live in herds, and . . ."

"He's lost on Planet Research again!" Zoe said, chuckling. She turned to face Erika. "Who do you think is doing this to the elephants? Could it be ivory poachers?"

"I don't think so," said Erika. "They're taking the heads, that's for sure, but ivory poachers only take the tusks, and never the flesh. I'm wondering if we've stumbled upon some illegal bush meat trade."

Zoe gasped. "People eat elephants?" she asked.

Erika nodded sadly.

"But why have they targeted Tomboi?" Zoe asked. "There's not much meat on a young elephant."

Erika began to speak, but Ben interrupted her. "This is awful!" he shouted, his eyes glued to the computer screen.

Zoe felt sick when she saw the website he was looking at. It was called Hunting Holidays International. Men with guns posed next to the bloody corpses of tigers, lions, elephants, rhinos, and buffalo. Ads down the sides of the web page encouraged the reader to have their trophy animal heads mounted by the organization's taxidermist.

"'Come face to face with nature in the wild,'" Zoe read aloud, struggling to get the words out. "'Your friends will be in awe of your bravery as you hunt down the fiercest animals in the world.'"

"My guess is trophy hunters have been hunting the elephants," said Ben.

Erika nodded. "It's possible," she said. "Hunting is illegal in Kenya, so it couldn't be done openly. But that doesn't mean it's not happening."

Zoe clicked through the photos on the hunting site. It was hard to look at the dead animals. The hunters were smiling proudly in the photos.

"The same faces keep showing up in these photos," Zoe said, pointing at the screen. "Look at that guy with the cheeks like a bulldog and pins all over his hat. It says his name is Frank Hall, president of the Big Game Hunters Club. He has shot animals on every continent." She clenched her teeth. "I can't believe someone would hunt a baby elephant."

Ben could tell his sister was upset. He shut off the monitor.

"The minute we get to Kenya, we're going to start investigating," he said to Zoe. "Our first stop is the Samburu village to find out whatever we can about Tomboi and his mother."

CHAPTER 3

SAMBURU NATIONAL PARK

Ben and Zoe hurried across the flagstoned courtyard of the Amani Lodge. The hotel was deep in the Samburu National Park and had every imaginable luxury. A fountain sparkled in the bright afternoon sun and guests lounged around the swimming pool under thatched umbrellas, sipping their drinks. Every now and then, black-faced monkeys darted across the floor in search of something to eat — until they were chased away by the waiters.

"It's pretty cool that we're staying somewhere so fancy," said Zoe, gazing around. "Look at all the rich tourists."

"We've got more important things to do," said Ben. "The village tour leaves in three minutes. Let's go."

Zoe walked faster. "I wonder if Erika's had any luck following up her lead."

They'd just checked in at the lodge when a message had come from WILD headquarters for Erika. It said that illegal bush meat was being sold in a town half a day's drive away. Erika had sped off in a rented jeep to see if it was linked to the slaughter of the elephants.

Ben glanced at Zoe nervously. "What are you talking about?" he said in a serious tone. "Our tutor is sick in bed, remember?"

"Of course!" Zoe said. She looked back and forth nervously to make sure no one had heard. "Sorry, I completely forgot about our cover story."

They climbed some steps to a lawn garden. Here and there, gazelles grazed on the short, cropped grass as if they were out on the plains.

"This is such a beautiful place," Zoe said. "It's hard to imagine that horrible things are happening to the elephants just a few miles away. I hope we can get some useful information from the Samburu. Where did the leaflet say the trip to the village started?"

"Here at the north garden," said Ben. "But I don't see anyone."

Ben ran to an older boy in an Amani Lodge uniform. He was weeding a flower bed. "Excuse me," Ben said. The boy looked up and grinned. He wore a staff name badge with RUNO on it. "Does the tour of the village leave from here?" Ben asked.

"Yes," said Runo. "It left two hours ago."

"Oh, no," Zoe said.

Ben checked his watch. His cheeks turned bright red. "Oops," he said. "I forgot to change my watch time."

"What should we do?" said Zoe. "We need to get to the village as soon as possible." Runo looked at Zoe, his eyes narrowed. "I mean, we were looking forward to going today," she said.

Runo put down his trowel. "Can you ride a camel?" he asked, his eyes dancing playfully.

"No," said Zoe.

"Yes!" said Ben, correcting his sister.

Zoe glared at her brother. "We've never ridden camels in our lives," she hissed.

Ben shrugged. "We're good horse riders," he said. "It can't be all that different, right?"

"I can get you camels right now," said Runo. "Your trip to the village will be fast."

"Great!" said Ben, getting out his wallet. "How much?"

"Nothing," said Runo. "But can you take a package of kitchen leftovers to my grandfather for his goats? He lives in the village. His name is Wambua." Before Ben or Zoe could respond, Runo turned and walked away. "Follow me."

* * *

Zoe's camel lurched from side to side. "I thought you said this would be easy," she said, gripping the front of the saddle. "It's nothing like horse riding at all."

"Just hold the reins and keep it steady,"
Ben said from atop his camel. "Runo said
these guys are very well trained. They
take tourists on daily rides to the village."

"I don't know if we're supposed to
take them out without a trainer," said
Zoe. "When we arrived at the camel
compound, Runo told us we had to keep it
a secret."

"It almost wasn't a secret after you let out that shriek!" teased Ben.

"I thought I was going to fall off when it stood up," Zoe said, glaring at Ben.

"It's fine when you get used to it," said Ben, smiling smugly. "And there's a great view from up here."

They gazed out over the amazing panorama of the Kenyan plain.

The flat landscape was broken up by clumps of bushes. Branches stretched like fans toward the clear, blue sky.

"There are animals everywhere!" Zoe said, pointing into the distance. "I see zebra, deer, and there's a massive herd of wildebeest."

"And giraffes are feeding on those trees!" added Ben.

A family of warthogs snuffled past, noses to the ground. "Aw, look at those sweet little piglets!" Zoe said.

Ben raised his eyebrows. "They're not so little," he teased.

They followed a beaten-down path through the yellow grass toward some distant dome-shaped huts. The huts were surrounded by a thick fence.

"I told you this would be easy," said Ben. "I'm going to ride faster."

Ben squeezed the camel's flanks with his legs. Nothing happened. He squeezed a bit harder. The camel gave a deep-throated snort and threw him off. Ben hit the ground in a cloud of dust.

Zoe burst out laughing.

"It's not funny!" Ben said, rubbing his lower back. His camel blinked its long lashes, then turned and continued to plod toward the village. "After you," Ben said, eyeing the camel warily. He started to follow on foot at a safe distance.

Finally, they reached the entrance to the village, which was just a narrow gap in the thorny fence. Zoe clicked her heels to make her camel kneel, and then she dismounted.

"That's a barrier to keep the elephants out," said Ben, pointing at the gate. "I read about it on the plane. The Samburu put it up to prevent the elephants from trampling their homes."

Zoe tied both camels securely to the fence. She tucked Wambua's package under her arm.

Zoe and Ben walked between the round huts. The walls were made of branches and the the floors were made of dried mud. Stretched skins and grass mats formed the domed roofs.

Women were cooking at pots over fires, and a nearby group of men were tending their goats. They all wore cloths wrapped around them like skirts, and strings of shiny beads dangled from their heads, necks, wrists, and ears. They looked up when they saw Ben and Zoe approaching, and then lowered their heads back to their tasks. No one greeted them, but some of the little kids stared, wide-eyed with curiosity.

"These people don't look very friendly," Zoe whispered to Ben.

"Maybe they're shy," Ben said. "Let's put in our translators."

Ben rummaged in his backpack and placed the small earpiece from the BUG in his ear. Zoe did the same. The two of them tried in vain to talk to villagers who passed, but they all scurried away without a word.

"Nobody wants to talk to us," said Zoe. "And what's really strange is they're not even talking to each other."

Zoe gasped. "Something bad happened here," she said, pointing at the blackened ruins of a nearby hut.

"Looks like a recent fire," said Ben.

"Here's another burned hut," said Zoe, pointing as they walked through the village. "And another. How strange. It can't have been one fire — the huts in between are untouched."

A woman holding a baby walked past. "Excuse me," said Zoe, holding up the parcel. "Wambua?"

The woman didn't look at her, but she hastily pointed toward a goat pen nearby. An old man was splashing water into a trough and the goats were nudging him. He spotted the package under Zoe's arm as the children approached him.

"From Runo," Zoe said with a smile.

"Thank you," said the old man. His face was painted with blue patterns and his earlobes were pulled down by heavy bead earrings. "Are you staying at the Amani lodge?"

"We're on vacation," said Zoe, glad to find someone ready to talk. "Our tutor sent us to find out all we can about elephants."

"They're such magnificent animals," added Ben. "Can you tell us more about them?"

The old man's face softened. "They are wonderful animals," he said. "We are blessed with a herd that lives on the plain. It is led by a matriarch called Nyeupe, which means 'white' in your language. She is much paler than the other elephants and is nearly fifty years old now."

He gestured for them to sit by a small fire. Nearby, a woman grinding corn in a wooden bowl gave them a nervous glance.

"Is her herd very big?" asked Zoe.

"Four grown females and two younger ones — you would call them teenagers, I suppose?" said Wambua. "And somewhere out there are two bull elephants. They do not live with the herd."

"Could you take us to them?" asked Ben.

For a moment Wambua's eyes lit up. "It is a wonderful trek," he said. "We walk for a day and make camp by the Tulivu waterhole at night. That way, we're ready to see the elephants when they come to drink at first light."

The woman suddenly called out to him in Samburu. Ben and Zoe heard her words translated through their earpieces.

"Be quiet, you foolish old man!" she warned. "Do you want to bring us even more trouble?"

Ben and Zoe forced themselves not to react. The woman sounded very frightened.

Wambua sighed heavily and shook his head. "I'm sorry, but we don't take visitors there anymore," he said sadly. He gave an involuntary glance over to the burnt huts.

Ben patted his pockets. "We'll pay well."

"I'm sorry, but it is just not possible," Wambua said flatly. "There is only one left, so it's not worth the trip, anyway." He stood. "Now I must tend to my goats. Goodbye."

Wambua turned to leave. "Thank you," Ben and Zoe said, then they began to walk back through the village.

A little girl came plodding across their path, waving her arm in front of her like an elephant's trunk. A little boy jumped up and followed the girl, pretending to be an elephant as well. He had a rope tied around his leg and was pretending to limp.

The limping boy spoke to the girl in Samburu. "Wait for me, Mom!" The translated words came through loud and clear. "My leg hurts."

"Come on, baby," said the girl. "We're falling behind."

Suddenly, two older boys rose up from behind a box, holding sticks to their shoulders like rifles.

Zoe and Ben exchanged shocked looks as they listened through their translator earpieces.

"Bang! Bang!" the two boys yelled. The two "elephants" fell to the ground.

Then they all started laughing. "Now I'll put a snare on your ankle," said the girl to one of the older boys. "And I will be one of the hunters this time."

The girl started to untie the rope from her friend's leg, but just then a woman came running over. The little girl froze, a guilty look on her face.

"Stop that!" cried the woman. "I've told you before. No more talk of elephants! You don't know who's listening. Remember what happened last week."

The woman gave Ben and Zoe a scared glance and ushered the smaller children inside a nearby hut.

"They were acting out a hunt!" Ben said to Zoe. "A hunt where young elephants were being snared to slow them down. They must have overheard their parents talking."

"The baby and its mother are separated from the herd, so they're easy to pick off," said Zoe, nodding.

"So hunters have snared poor Tomboi to catch his mother," Ben said, "and the adult villagers seem too frightened to even talk about it."

"I wonder if the burned huts are connected with this," said Zoe. "After all, something's stopping the villagers from even mentioning the elephants."

Ben clenched his fists. "Then we'll have to protect the herd for them," he said.

CHAPTER 4

FRANK HALL

The sun was low over the plain by the time Ben and Zoe got back to the lodge. Runo quickly snuck their camels back to the compound.

"We have to set off to find Tomboi tomorrow," said Ben as they made their way back to their room. "Wambua said the herd goes to the waterhole at sunrise. If we leave early in the morning and camp out overnight, we should get there at the right time."

"The sooner we fix his leg, the better," said Zoe. "We don't know when the hunt is going to be, but if we can heal Tomboi, then he won't be trailing the herd. Then the hunters will find it much harder to get him and his mom."

As they crossed the lobby to collect their key from the reception desk, Zoe stopped and grabbed her brother's arm. "Do you recognize that man leaning on the desk?" she said.

Ben studied the tall, plump man who was talking loudly in English to the hotel manager. "No," Ben said.

"Look at his hat with all the pins and feathers on it," said Zoe. "We saw enough photos of him wearing it on that awful hunting site."

"Oh, yeah!" said Ben. "It's that idiot who boasted he'd shot game on every continent."

"What was his name?" asked Zoe. "It was all over the site."

Ben thought for a minute. "Hall!" he said. "Frank Hall."

They got their key and let themselves into their bedroom.

"It can't be a coincidence that a big-game hunter turns up where elephants are being shot illegally," Ben said as he paced up and down between the two beds. "But we don't have any proof that he's here for that reason."

"Which is where Uncle Stephen's OWL comes in," said Zoe. "We can plant it on Mr. Hall. Then we'll see — and hear — if he's up to anything." She took out the box that contained the OWL from her backpack and opened it. "There's only one problem. When are we going to get the chance to attach it to him?"

Ben frowned. "Why not right now?" he asked.

"We can't just go up to him and slap it on his shirt!" said Zoe. "Besides, he won't be wearing the same clothes every day."

They thought for a moment.

"Maybe his hat?" Ben said. "He seems to always wear it."

"Good idea!" said Zoe. She slipped the little box into the pocket of her shorts. "But finding the right moment is going to be difficult."

"We can figure that out over dinner," said Ben. "I'm starving."

Zoe rolled her eyes. "Do boys ever stop thinking about food?" she said.

CHAPTER 5
LESTER HALL

Ben and Zoe sat at a table on the
wooden deck of the restaurant. Their table
overlooked a small lake. Citronella candles
burned brightly, keeping the mosquitoes at
bay. The sun had gone down behind the
low hills to the west, leaving a warm glow
on the horizon.

Occasionally, a security guard passed by
the restaurant, rifle slung over his shoulder,
watching in case any predators came too
close to the restaurant.

A few moments later, a nocturnal animal was spotted coming for a drink at the lake. "What's that?" said Zoe as a small creature with a bushy black-and-white striped tail crept up to the water's edge.

Ben got out his BUG and began to fiddle with it under the table. "Genet cat," he said. "Though it's not actually a cat, but rather a member of the mongoose family."

"It's so cute," said Zoe. Ben groaned.

They ate their fish curry as slowly as possible so they could watch the diners come and go.

After about an hour, Ben was getting full, and Zoe was picking at her food, and there was still no sign of Frank Hall.

Ben took out his BUG again. "The BUG has identified caracal cries," he told Zoe, eyes shining. "You know, those lynx-like cats with the amazing pointed ears?"

Zoe was about to respond when a voice interrupted them. "Cool videogame you've got there." Ben looked up. A boy with short blond hair was grinning at them from the next table. "Have you played Call of War 4?" As the boy came closer to them, Ben quickly pressed a button so a videogame would flash up on the BUG's screen.

"No, I only have a football game so far," Ben said, showing the boy the screen. "It's not much fun." He slid the BUG quickly into his pocket.

"I don't think we'll be playing many games, anyway," said Zoe. "There's too much to see."

"It's great here, isn't it?" said the boy eagerly. "I got a new camera and I can't wait to try it out. We're going on a trek later this week to photograph the wildlife. I'm hoping to get the big five. Lions, elephants, rhinos, and buffalo will be easy, but leopards are rare."

"Making friends, Lester?" boomed a voice behind them.

Lester stood straight up and frowned. "Just chatting, Dad," he said quietly.

Ben and Zoe looked to see who'd spoken. It was Frank Hall.

The big-game hunter flung his jacket on the back of his chair and sat down with a loud grunt. Lester seemed embarrassed.

"I was just talking about our trek," Lester explained, sitting back down at his own table. He nervously fidgeted with the flowers in the vase at their table.

"You'll be part of a real man's world for a change," said his father. "Walking the plain, roughing it in a tent, cooking your own food —" He stopped as Lester let out a wail of horror and backed away from the flowers.

"What's the matter?" asked Mr. Hall.

"A spider," cried Lester. "A great big one is on that petal!"

Red with anger, Mr. Hall knocked the spider onto the table and squashed it with his fist. "You could at least pretend to be tough," he grumbled, flicking the spider carcass away.

Lester's cheek flushed red. He looked down at his feet. Ben and Zoe pretended not to notice. "Poor Lester," whispered Zoe. "His dad is terrible."

"Whatever else Mr. Hall's up to," said Ben, "at least he's taking his son on a photography expedition. Maybe that's the only reason he's here."

"We need to be sure," said Zoe, patting the pocket that contained her OWL. "Look, he doesn't have his hat with him right now."

"Then his hat has to be back in his room," said Ben.

"We can't go in there," whispered Zoe.

"We have to," said Ben. "And for that we need the key. I can see the keychain sticking out of his jacket pocket. I'll distract him while you grab it."

"Be careful," warned Zoe.

Ben got to his feet and winked. "Trust me," he said. He strode past the Halls and walked to the dessert table. He placed two papayas and a mango on his plate, and made his way back to the table. Just as he reached Lester and his father, he pretended to trip. The fruit rolled off the plate and bounced undernearth their table.

"Oops!" Ben said. He kneeled beneath the tablecloth and picked up the lost fruit.

"What are you doing?" growled Frank Hall, peering under the table.

Ben rolled the mango across the floor toward Zoe. She leaped from her seat and grabbed for it on the ground. At the same time, she slipped her other hand into Mr. Hall's jacket pocket and removed the key.

Zoe slid the key up her shirt sleeve just as Ben emerged from under the table. "Got them!" he said, holding the papayas.

"And here's the mango!" said Zoe, producing the fruit. "I'm sorry we interrupted your meal."

Lester started to talk, but caught his father's glance and stopped. "Dreadful behavior!" growled Frank Hall. "You shouldn't be allowed in here on your own. Where are your parents?"

"Our parents aren't with us," said Zoe.

"Disgraceful!" Mr. Hall said. "Kids all on their own."

Lester looked down at the table in embarrassment.

"But our tutor's in her room," Ben said calmly. "She's not feeling well."

"Why didn't you have your meal with her?" said Mr. Hall. "Then you wouldn't have bothered the rest of us."

"We're going there now," Zoe said quickly. "This fruit's for her." She grabbed her brother by the arm. "Come on, Ben."

CHAPTER 6

UNDERCOVER

After checking to make sure the hall was empty, Zoe turned the key to room 212. The door swung open to reveal a huge bedroom. All around the walls were beautiful paintings of lions, leopards and giraffes in their natural surroundings. The two of them snuck inside and shut the door.

"Wow!" said Ben. "This is a lot nicer than our room."

On a desk in the corner sat a laptop and some hunting magazines. In the middle of the bed was Mr. Hall's hat.

"There it is," said Zoe nervously. She threw the key and the mango on the bed and picked up the hat. She quickly positioned the OWL on the front, between a green feather and a button. Within seconds it was stuck. Just as she set the hat back on the bed, they heard voices outside the door.

"I'm certain I had the key with me," Mr. Hall said.

"It is not a problem, sir," said the voice of the receptionist. "I have the master key with me." A moment later, they heard a key sliding into the lock.

"Quick," whispered Ben. "Hide!"

Ben and Zoe slid under the bed.

"The mango!" said Zoe. "It's still on the bed!"

Zoe scrambled out and retrieved the piece of fruit. Then she quickly slid back underneath the bed just before the door creaked open.

They saw Mr. Hall's sandaled feet striding toward them. Then he stopped. The children looked at each other nervously, their eyes wide. Had they been spotted?

Frank Hall let out a gruff laugh. "Here it is!" he said. He walked to the bed. His feet were only inches from their faces. There was a rattle as he picked up the key, then the clink of a few coins. He moved away from the bed. "Take that for your trouble," he said to the receptionist.

"Thank you, sir," the other man said. The door closed softly as the receptionist left with his tip.

"Can we stay here and watch TV?" Lester asked Mr. Hall. "I'm tired."

"We didn't come all this way for you to watch television," said his father. "We're going to talk to Chitundu now. He wants to have a good look at the hunting badges." He picked up his hat and put it on.

"Who's Chitundu?" Lester asked.

"I told you about him. Don't you ever listen?" said Mr. Hall, sighing. "He's a Samburu from the local village, but he lives at the hotel now. He's the one taking us on this expedition."

"I remember now," muttered Lester. "Won't he be too busy to see us? You said he works as a chef here, and dinner's still being served."

"He'll be there," said Mr. Hall. "But we can't let anyone know that he's involved with our trip. If the lodge found out he was helping us, he'd get in big trouble. Their employees aren't supposed to make extra money from the guests."

"So how can Chitundu come with us without the lodge knowing about it?" asked Lester.

"Use your head, son," said his father.
"He's taking a few days off — unpaid, of
course — so they won't know anything
about it. But he'll get more than enough
money from me to make up for his lost
wages."

Mr. Hall moved toward the door. "Let's
go," he said. "And bring your camera to
show Chitundu."

Lester sighed. His hurried footsteps
walked around the room, and then back to
join his father. Finally the door clicked shut.
Ben and Zoe waited for a moment before
they slid out from their hiding place.

Ben grinned. "I thought I was going to
squash the papayas," he said. "Shame to
ruin our dessert —" He broke off when he
heard a key turning in the lock again.

Zoe and Ben barely had time to hide under the bed again before Lester ran in.

"I'm going downstairs, Lester," said Mr. Hall's grumbling voice from the hall. "Be quick about it."

"I will," Lester called back. "I just need my camera battery."

Ben and Zoe heard Lester unzip a bag. He fumbled with the camera and the battery dropped to the wooden floor with a clatter. It bounced and slid right under the bed, coming to rest between Ben and Zoe.

They shrank as far away as they could. Lester got down on his knees. They held their breaths. They were going to be discovered.

CHAPTER 7

CHITUNDU

Ben quickly rolled on to his back, pulled out his BUG, and swiftly tapped the keys.

As Lester's hand felt farther under the bed, the sound of a hissing snake burst out from Ben's BUG. Lester gave a terrified cry and quickly withdrew his hand. They saw his feet rushing in a mad panic to the door.

It slammed shut behind him. Zoe let out a sigh of relief. "How did you know Lester was scared of snakes?" she asked.

Ben shrugged as he pulled himself out from his hiding place. "A lucky guess," he said. "I remembered how scared he was of the spider."

"We'd better go before Mr. Hall sends someone to get rid of the snake," said Zoe.

Back in their own room, Ben threw the papayas onto the dressing table. "This trek seems to be real top-secret," he said. "What if we're right about the hunt? Why all the secrecy if they're just going on a photography expedition?"

"Slow down, agent Ben!" teased Zoe. "Neither of them mentioned a hunt. All we know is Chitundu's not supposetd to be doing extra work while he's employed at the lodge. And Lester took his camera to show him. It might just be a photography expedition."

"Let's listen in on the OWL," said Ben. He tapped the OWL key on his BUG. The screen flickered, and then revealed an image of glowing lights, palm trees, and tables.

"They're in the corner of the courtyard," said Zoe, looking over her brother's shoulder. "There doesn't seem to be anyone sitting near them. But I can't see if they're with this Chitundu person. Can you hear anything?"

"I could if you'd be quiet!" said Ben.

Zoe stuck her tongue out at him.

The children sat on Zoe's bed in silence, listening. At first all they could make out was the murmur of voices. Then the screen was blocked by a green Amani Lodge uniform.

"Hello, Chitundu," they heard Mr. Hall say.

"Sit down," the other man said. "I only have a moment." His voice was quiet and had an accent similar to Runo's. "My boss is around somewhere."

"He won't have anything to complain about," Mr. Hall said. "After all, you're simply telling us the recipe for that delicious Nyama Choma we had tonight, aren't you?" Mr. Hall sounded like he was in a great mood. He lowered his voice. "This is my son, Lester. He'll be coming with us. Is everything ready?"

"It is," Chitundu said. "I have the . . . equipment ready, and I can take some time off in three days."

The speaker leaned forward, his hands pressed onto the table.

Now Ben and Zoe could see Chitundu's face on their BUG screen. He was young, with very short black hair.

"I am pleased to meet you, Lester," he said. He pointed to something on the table and his smile widened. "I see you have your camera. It's very nice, but I will bring something else to help you with your . . . shots."

The image swung around to show Lester examining his camera. "Cheer up, boy!" said his father.

Lester still looked sullen.

"Bah," his father said, waving his hand dismissively. "Go get yourself a lemonade while Chitundu and I talk."

Lester scraped back his seat and walked away. As soon as he'd gone, Mr. Hall turned back to face Chitundu.

"I hope you have something to help my shots, too," he said slyly. "You know, since I wasn't able to bring my own."

Chitundu looked around to make sure that no one was in earshot. "Of course," he answered smoothly. "This is the highest velocity I could get, and it will go through bone like it's butter. I have hidden it near the waterhole so you won't be seen carrying it there. Of course, I will have to carry something to protect us, but that won't arouse any suspicion."

Ben and Zoe tensed. They listened intently to the OWL. "And the calf will be very slow by then," Chitundu went on, smiling smugly. "It has been days since I snared him, so he and his mother will be well behind the herd."

"So he's the one behind the elephant killings!" Ben said through gritted teeth.

"It's just like how the children in the village were playing," added Zoe.

"I'll get the mother," Mr. Hall said. He sounded very pleased with himself. "And Lester gets the youngster. It'll be his first kill. But remember, it's to stay a surprise for him until we're nearly to the waterhole."

"I will not forget," said Chitundu gravely. "And remember our agreement. You get the heads, I get the meat."

"Of course," said Mr. Hall.

"That's just awful!" Zoe said, punching her pillow in anger.

Chitundu was getting up to leave. "I have to get back to the kitchen," he said.

"Thank you for the recipe," said Mr. Hall loudly. "I know it's going to be a success."

The screen suddenly swung to face Lester, who was approaching with his lemonade. "I thought you said my camera was really good, Dad," he said. "Why does Chitundu want to give me a different one?"

"That was just a joke," his father said quickly. "Remember, Chitundu's an expert at this sort of thing. I think he has a special zoom lens you can borrow. So stop whining!"

Ben shut off the OWL. "Now we know who our hunters are!" he said. "And we've got three days before they set off to track down Tomboi and his mom."

Ben checked the satellite map on his BUG. "The waterhole Wambua told us about is southeast of here," he told his sister. "He said it was a day's walk, so if we leave before first light tomorrow like we planned, we'll arrive at the waterhole well ahead of time."

Zoe began to stuff the sleeping bags and food rations in their backpacks to get ready for the trek. "Do you think Tomboi will have the chance to recover and rejoin the herd?" she asked worriedly. "You know, so the hunters won't be able to track him down again after he's healed?"

"I hope so," Ben said.

Ben picked up his BUG. "I'll report to Uncle Stephen," he said. "Since we now know the hunting party will be setting out in three days, he can alert the authorities. That will give them plenty of time to catch them in the act."

"Good idea," Zoe said. She watched as Ben pressed the key on his BUG that put him straight through to WILD HQ.

"Have any news?" asked their uncle's eager voice.

Ben quickly told him about planting the OWL, then reported everything they'd heard. "So you'll get the Kenya Wildlife Service to arrest the hunters?" Ben asked.

"It's not so easy, Ben," Uncle Stephen replied. "This Chitundu fellow is quite clever. There's no evidence linking him to the hunt, and we can't just tell anyone that you heard the conversation through WILD equipment."

"Then what should we do?" Ben asked.

"Once you've helped Tomboi, keep tracking Hall's movements and let me know when the hunters are getting near the waterhole," their uncle's voice said. "I'll make sure the Kenya Wildlife Service hears about it in time. Over and out."

Zoe stuffed the medical kit, torches, water bottles, night-vision goggles, and binoculars into the backpacks.

"The tranquilizer guns are on the top, just in case," Zoe said, zipping up the bags. "Hopefully we won't need them."

Ben smiled. "Better safe than sorry," he said, nodding.

"Here we come, Tomboi!" Zoe said.

CHAPTER 8

ON THE HUNT

Zoe woke to the sound of her alarm buzzing in her ear. She staggered out of bed in the dark and shook Ben. He was always hard to wake up, especially at five thirty in the morning. By the time he'd pulled on his clothes, his sister was ready by the door.

They crept down the dim corridor, trying not to make the wooden floor creak. At last, the big double doors at the front of the lobby came into view.

"I can't see anyone at the desk," said Zoe. Let's —" Just then, someone came around the corner and ran right into her. It was Lester Hall. He had his camera hanging around his neck, and he looked like he'd put his clothes on in a hurry.

"Sorry," he mumbled, scratching his tousled head. "I'm not completely awake yet."

"And we thought we were the only ones up!" said Ben, trying to sound relaxed and friendly. "Going somewhere cool?"

Lester yawned. "My dad's taking me on a photo expedition," he said. "But I didn't think he'd be dragging me out of bed in the middle of the night!"

Ben and Zoe stared at him, trying to keep the look of shock from their faces.

The hunt was leaving today!

"What are you two doing up so early?" came Mr. Hall's voice as he strode into view.

He wore state-of-the-art hiking boots, expensive binoculars, and his decorated safari hat.

Mr. Hall looked Ben and Zoe up and down, eyeing their backpacks. He poked a finger at them. "I get it," he said. "You're sneaking out while your tutor's asleep. I bet she'd like to know what you're up to."

"No," said Zoe. "We —"

"I'm telling the hotel that you two are heading off on your own!" Mr. Hall interrupted. "They won't want to send out a search party when a pair of stupid kids get eaten by lions."

"Our tutor's coming with us," Ben said. "She's better now. We're just waiting for her here."

"She knows this area well," Zoe said, taking up Ben's improvised story. "She lived here when she was a girl." She could feel her heart thumping. Would Mr. Hall believe their cover story?

Mr. Hall let out a grunt. "All right, then," he said. A brief look of concern flickered over his face. "Where exactly are you going?"

Ben thought quickly. "To the village," he said. "Our tutor wants us to experience a day in the life of a villager."

Mr. Hall forced a thin smile. He seemed to be relieved that they wouldn't be going in his direction. "Come on, Lester," he said. "Let's get going. I've ordered us some breakfast. We've got a long hike ahead, so we'll need the energy."

The yawning boy left with his dad.

"This is a disaster!" whispered Zoe. "We thought we'd have three days before the hunters left. Why have they changed their plans all of a sudden?"

"Don't worry about that now," said Ben. "Our mission is to save Tomboi, and that means getting there before the hunters."

"And letting Uncle Stephen know that the hunt is on so he can alert the Kenya Wildlife Service," added Zoe. "Come on, we can tell him on the way."

Dawn was just breaking and the air was still cold as Ben and Zoe snuck across the spotlit lodge grounds. They hid behind a hippopotamus statue as an armed security guard walked past.

"We have to find a new route," said Ben. "And that's going to be hard. You can see a long way on the plain because it's so flat. We'll be spotted if we're anywhere near the hunting party." He brought up a satellite picture of the area. A red light pulsed over the lodge. "They're in the dining room."

"Let's hope it's a huge breakfast that takes them a long time to eat," said Zoe.

"And that Frank Hall will be so full he'll hardly be able to walk," Ben said. He zoomed out until the waterhole appeared on the map. "I know we should be heading southeast," he muttered, "but if we go southwest, there's more cover."

"You're right," Zoe said. She looked over her shoulder. "There are clumps of trees there." She pointed. "And there."

"Then we cut southeast through that outcrop of rocks and finally get to the undergrowth near the waterhole," said Ben. "That's a good hiding place to wait for the elephants tomorrow morning. We'll camp somewhere along the way."

"But we'll have to move fast," said Zoe. "Now our trek will be longer than theirs."

Ben tapped away at some keys on his BUG. "I've sent a message to Uncle Stephen to let him know the change of plans," he said.

"Tranquilizer guns are ready," added Zoe, nodding toward a large sign that read DO NOT PROCEED UNACCOMPANIED BEYOND THIS POINT. "And keep your scent dispersers active so we don't smell tempting to predators."

When the coast was clear, they slipped out of the lodge grounds. Ben checked the map on his BUG and gestured for Zoe to follow.

Skirting around the lodge, Ben and Zoe took in the spectacular view of the plain bathed in the early morning sun. The flat land stretched across the landscape toward the snow-capped Mount Kenya in the far distance.

Tall, fanned acacias and thick-trunked baobabs dotted the land. The children moved quickly, darting for cover behind the trees wherever they could. As the sun began to warm the arid land, the plain woke up. Herds of zebra and wildebeest began to graze on the open grass, and giraffes galloped along as if chasing each other.

"Look, over there," said Ben. "It's our first elephant!"

"It's huge!" said Zoe, wide-eyed. "It couldn't be part of our herd, could it?"

"It's a male," said Ben. "Wambua told us they live alone, remember?"

The bull elephant stamped around, his head jerking left and right and his trunk swinging irritably.

"He looks like he has a temper," said Zoe. "Good thing we're nowhere near him."

Ben came to a sudden halt. "What's that over there?" he said, pointing at the far distance. "Something's moving to the east, and I don't think it's an animal." He threw himself flat on the ground, pulling Zoe down with him.

Zoe grabbed her binoculars and focused them. "It's the hunting party," she said. "We were in full view."

"That was close!" said Ben. "Did they see us?"

"I'll find out," said Zoe, turning on her OWL.

"I did see something," they heard Mr. Hall insist. "It looked like people."

"I can't see anything," came Chitundu's voice. "I'm sure it was just an animal."

"I hope so, Chitundu," grunted Mr. Hall. "For your sake."

"Now that we've stopped, can I take some photos?" asked Lester. "We've been going so fast I haven't managed to take any yet."

"You'll get some good shots later," his father said with a chuckle.

"We have to be more careful," said Zoe. She studied the map on her BUG. "We should go farther west."

They took the new route, hiding behind high grass and bushes whenever possible.

Suddenly, there was a tremendous crashing in the bushes ahead of them as the bull elephant burst onto the open plain. He stamped his front feet, blowing angrily through his trunk. Ben and Zoe stopped, not daring to move.

"Stay still," whispered Ben. "He might ignore us."

The elephant growled and shook his head. Then he raised his trunk and gave a tremendous trumpet of rage.

The elephant pounded toward them, his huge ears outstretched. "Run!" Zoe cried.

CHAPTER 9

PROWLER

Ben caught his sister's arm as she turned to flee. "Just step into the thick bushes," he said quietly. "Move slowly and don't make eye contact."

Zoe hesitated, but soon followed Ben. She had to try hard not to check over her shoulder at the charging mammal nearby.

The sound of thundering feet grew closer. Leaves and branches flew into the air as the bull elephant pushed through the bushes toward the twins' hiding place.

Then, as quickly as it had started, the thudding stopped. The elephant was standing a short distance away, tossing his head back and forth while snorting. At last he rushed off, his trunk swinging.

"It was just a fake charge," said Ben.

"How did you know?" Zoe asked.

"He had his ears forward," Ben said. "Anyone who knows anything about elephants could have told you that."

Zoe glared at him. Ben managed to keep a straight face for about five seconds, then he burst out laughing. "Okay, okay — I read about it on the plane," he admitted. "Ears forward and a lot of noise means the elephant is just showing us who's boss. It's when his ears are back and he's silent that you should be worried."

Ben scratched his chin thoughtfully. "Kinda like how you get real quiet when you're angry, I guess," he joked. Zoe gave him a friendly punch in the shoulder.

Soon, they reached an outcropping of rocks that pushed up through the grass.

"Lunch time," said Ben, sitting under the welcome shade of an overhanging tree. He unwrapped an energy bar.

"They've stopped too," said Zoe, watching the screen on her BUG.

Mr. Hall was devouring a plateful of food. They saw each time he dipped his head to shovel in another forkful.

For a moment, Lester came into shot. He was toying miserably with the food on his plate. "Tell him what we have in store for tomorrow, Chitundu," barked Mr. Hall. "That'll bring a smile to his face."

Chitundu came into view, squatting a little way from his guests. He looked pleased with himself. "We will make camp tonight," he began. "At first light tomorrow, we will reach the elephants where they go to drink. I have lamed a calf by throwing a snare at his ankle. It's cutting into his leg and slowing him down."

Zoe clenched her teeth as she listened. Chitundu continued to outline his plan. "His mother will not leave him behind, so they are gradually getting farther behind the herd. It will be easy for your father to shoot her. She is a magnificent beast with good tusks."

"Excellent!" came Mr. Hall's voice. "She'll have a place of honor in my hallway."

"What do you mean?" came an angry shout. Lester was staring at his father, a look of shock on his face. "You didn't say you were going to shoot anything! Aren't we here to photograph the animals up close?"

"Well," Mr. Hall said, "afterward, you can take all the pictures you want of me standing over my kill!" He laughed.

"I don't want to hunt!" Lester said. "I've told you many times, but you never listen. It's illegal here in Kenya, anyway!"

"That makes it more of a thrill," came Mr. Hall's voice. "Anyway, Chitundu's taken care of all that. Haven't you?"

"Yes, sir," Chitundu said. He was grinning at Mr. Hall.

"No one suspects a thing," said Mr. Hall. "Although I did wonder why you moved the trek up three days. There aren't any problems, I hope."

"None," said Chitundu. "The only reason we set out this morning is because I had to change my time off with one of the other chefs."

"What about the Samburu?" asked Mr. Hall. "Do they know what's going on?"

"They will not bother us," Chitundu said, smirking. "I have been doing this for a while now. The people in my village claim to have some stupid bond with the elephants and there were protests at first, but I got some friends to pay them a visit. A few huts got burned, and they learned the errors of their ways."

Zoe turned to Ben. "So that's what happened at the Samburu village," she said.

Ben nodded. "It certainly explains why the tribespeople were so frightened."

Lester spoke. "This is awful, Dad," he said. He'd come up close to his father. "I don't want anything to do with it."

"Don't be a wimp!" Mr. Hall said. "We've got a special treat for you. Don't we, Chitundu?"

"I have a gun especially for your height and weight," Chitundu said to Lester. "The young calf will be barely be able to move now with that bad leg of his. He will be a perfectly easy first kill for you."

"I don't like it," Lester said, his voice quavering. "I don't want to kill anything, Dad!"

"You need to toughen up, son," Mr. Hall said roughly. "And I know just how to do it. I'll give you a boxing lesson. Stand and face me."

"I don't want to," Lester said, shrinking away.

"Nonsense!" Mr. Hall said. 'Take a swing!"

"No!" Lester cried. "Leave me alone —"

"Put your fists up, boy!" came Mr. Hall's challenge. He lunged at his son. Just then, the scene on the BUG shook and spun.

Zoe gasped. "His hat fell off," she said. She and Ben got a sudden view of a huge boot sole. Then there was a nasty crunching sound and the screen went black. They looked at each other in horror.

"He stepped on it!" cried Ben. "He broke the OWL."

"This is really bad," said Zoe. "We can't keep track of them now."

"Then we're going to have to pick up our pace," said Ben. "I'll message Uncle Stephen to let him know we've lost our link."

* * *

By nightfall, Ben and Zoe were exhausted. They'd ignored their aching legs and lungs and pushed on until the sun was a huge orange ball on the horizon. The heat of the day was already beginning to fade.

"We should stop," said Ben. "We need some sleep."

"But there's no shelter here," said Zoe.

"Look over there at that small hill,"
Ben said. "It's not far. We can rest in our
sleeping bags and still see across the plain."

"We won't be able to light a fire up
there, though. It'll be seen," said Zoe.
"Good thing our sleeping bags are warm."

When they reached the little hill, Ben
took out the ultra-thin sleeping bags, a
clever invention of their uncle's. He and
Zoe made themselves as comfortable as
they could on the hard ground.

Zoe handed Ben an energy bar. Ben
made a sour face. "Just pretend it's a burger
and fries," she said, grinning. "Followed by
chocolate ice cream."

"I wish," said Ben.

After eating, they lay down, listening to
the manic call of the laughing hyenas.

Ben checked his BUG. "Just making sure the scent disperser's still on," he said. "Most of the predators around here like to hunt at night."

Zoe stared up at the thousands of stars that were sharp and bright against the deep black sky. Eventually, she fell into a troubled sleep, and dreamt of guns and dying elephants.

* * *

"Zoe!" Ben's voice startled her awake.

"What?" Zoe said, starting to sit up.

"Don't move!" Ben said.

Ben was lying stock still beside her. It was very dark and her breath came out in clouds in the cold air. And then she saw it. An even darker shape padding around their backpacks, almost close enough to touch. They had a visitor — a huge lioness.

CHAPTER 10

TOMBOI

Ben and Zoe listened to the lioness as she prowled around them. She padded up and down, pushing at their backpacks with her nose. One tipped over. The lioness sprang back, snarling. Zoe's eyes flickered with terror, but she didn't dare move.

Soon, the lioness moved out of sight, but they could still hear a strange scratching sound. Then a *beep* rang out. Zoe's heart sank. She realized that the lioness must be pawing at her BUG.

If she damaged it, the scent disperser
might stop working. Then she'd be sure
to catch their scent. Zoe could feel panic
rising in her chest. *Remember your WILD
training*, she told herself. *Don't move. Slow,
shallow breathing.*

Ben lay still. He saw that Zoe was worried sick, but there was nothing he could do. Now the lioness's huge head came into his view, looming over him. He closed his eyes as her muzzle grew closer and closer to his face. He could feel her hot breath. The smell of blood filled his nostrils as her nose touched his cheek. It was strange how gentle this ferocious animal was being, considering it could kill him at any moment.

Then they heard a distant, bleating sound. The lioness whipped around and sped off toward it. Alarmed cries and the pounding of hooves filled the air.

For a moment, neither Ben nor Zoe moved. At last they sat up and stared anxiously into the dark, looking for any signs of the lioness returning.

Ben reached out for Zoe's BUG. "Yuck, it has lion slobber on it," he said. "At least it's still working."

"I was so frightened," Zoe said shakily. "I couldn't stop shaking, and nearly gave us away."

Her brother put his arm round her. "You just avoided being eaten by the top predator in Africa," he said. "I think it's okay to be a little scared."

Zoe gave him a big smile. "I wish I could thank whatever animal it was that made that noise," she said.

"Agreed," Ben said. "But I bet it has its hooves full with that hungry lioness."

Zoe frowned at the thought of an animal being eaten. "Let's get going," she said, changing the subject.

Zoe pulled out their small, lightweight night-vision goggles and handed a pair to Ben.

Ben nodded and opened a cereal bar. "You can't be hungry already!" said Zoe. "It's only four o'clock!"

Ben grinned. "An early breakfast," he said. He bit into the bar and chewed noisily.

The night world turned bright green as they put on their goggles. They walked as softly as possible between the clearly defined trees and deep grasses, checking the satellite map as they traveled.

A strange noise rang out from nearby. "What's that sound?" asked Ben, clutching at Zoe's backpack strap. "It sounds like hissing."

Zoe pointed. "Look, the ground is moving!" she said.

The children backed away. A wide column of ants was marching along, completely blocking their path. It stretched endlessly in both directions. The ants scrambled over sticks and leaves in their way, not stopping for an instant.

"They must be the soldier ants of the colony," whispered Zoe, pointing down at them. "They're as long as my finger."

Ben tapped a key on his BUG and held it toward the writhing mass of insects. The hissing sound was even louder now.

"At least it wasn't a snake," said Zoe. "Can we get through them?"

Her brother shook his head. "'Dorylus,'" he read. "Also known as safari ants."

At that moment a large stray centipede scuttled toward the column. The nearest ants immediately swarmed all over it. Soon it stopped moving. Its body was eaten by the ants within seconds.

Zoe shuddered. "We'd better wait until they're gone," she said quietly.

Ben laughed. "There are millions of them," he said, shrugging his shoulders. "We'll be here for days."

"If only those acacia trees were growing closer to each other," said Zoe. "We could use them as a bridge."

"And if there were vines, we could do a Tarzan swing right over the ants," said Ben. "No point wasting any more time," Zoe said. "Maybe we can get across farther ahead."

They trudged alongside the ants, keeping a safe distance. They watched as careless insects were engulfed and eaten in a flash by the ants.

They could see the wide column of ants weaving its way across the rough open ground into the dark distance. "It's like they have their route and they're going to stick to it," said Ben.

"This isn't working," said Zoe, checking the map on the BUG. "They're heading south now and we need to go east. They're pushing us off our route. We have to cross them somehow or we won't get to the waterhole in time."

Ben shrugged. "All we can do is keep walking," he said.

"Look!" Zoe said. "The trees here are growing closer together. Follow me."

Zoe grasped the trunk of the nearest tree and pulled herself up into its branches. Ben could see that its branches crossed with the branches of a smaller tree, which was on the other side of the ant column.

Soon, Zoe was hanging by her arms from a high branch. It shook dangerously as she moved. Then she leaned out and grabbed a branch from the smaller tree. "Here goes!" she said.

The branch sunk under her weight as she swung onto it. For a moment, she thought she was going to lose her grip. She glanced down at the writhing river of ants, remembering what had happened to the centipede.

Knuckles white, she held on tightly, traveling hand over hand until she reached the other side.

She jumped to the ground, a look of triumph on her face. "I did it!" she called to Ben.

Ben climbed up the trunk and edged across until he was hanging from the smaller tree. Then the branch began to creak ominously.

"Hurry!" called Zoe. "It's going to break!"

"I'm almost there," Ben said as he scurried along.

A loud crack split the air as the branch tore away from the trunk. Ben plummeted downward, kicking madly to land clear of the column of deadly insects. He rolled over as he landed and stood up quickly.

"That was close!" he said. Then he leaped up and grabbed his arm. "Ow!"

Zoe could see a large ant on Ben's elbow. Then she spotted two more, higher up his arm. She slapped them off his skin, leaving dark marks behind. Ben yelped each time she hit him.

"It's okay now," she said. "They're gone."

"Thanks," said Ben, examining the bites. "I think they left their teeth behind, though."

Zoe turned her flashlight on. Stuck deep in Ben's skin were three sets of tiny ant fangs. She tried to pull them out, but Ben yanked his arm away with a cry. "It's too painful," he said. "Anyway, there's no time for this now."

Zoe ignored him and took out the first-aid kit from her backpack. She scanned the labels in the torchlight.

"Analgesic cream," Zoe said, unscrewing the lid. "It'll take away the pain." She rubbed it on to his arm. Ben winced, but let her do it. Then they set off again.

Just as the first rays of dawn were spreading over the ground, Ben and Zoe emerged from the trees. They took off their night-vision goggles and packed them away. Within a few minutes, the sun was completely clear of the horizon. Birds started to sing and a group of baboons began to swing from tree to tree above Ben and Zoe. A herd of buffalo meandered by, and a group of impalas chewed peacefully, watching them pass.

Beyond was the white-capped peak of the distant mountain. And in front of them was the waterhole, rippling gently in the sunlight.

"We made it!" said Ben. "And we beat the hunters here."

"And look — the herd is coming!" said Zoe.

The children crouched in the dense undergrowth, watching the line of elephants lumber toward the pool's edge.

Ben pointed at a huge, pale-looking elephant with extra baggy skin. "That must be Nyeupe, the matriarch, up in front," he whispered.

"I can't see a calf, so Tomboi and his mother must be way behind," said Zoe.

The matriarch gave a snort and waded into the pool. Others followed, sucking up the water and squirting it into their mouths.

Zoe sighed with delight as two of the elephants on the bank entwined their trunks playfully around each other. "That's absolutely adorable!" she said.

"No time for cuteness overload!" warned Ben. "We still have to find Tomboi and his mom. They must be coming from the same direction as the rest did. If we go around the northern edge of the water, over there behind the thickest trees, we should be able to intercept them as they try to catch up with the herd."

Slowly as they could, they made their way for the bushes where the elephants had come from. "This has to be their regular route," said Ben, staring at the path through the trees. "Look how the ground's been beaten down."

"Tomboi must be in real trouble with that snare," whispered Zoe. "I don't see him anywhere. What if it's already infected?"

Just then, Ben's BUG vibrated. "It's Uncle Stephen," he said.

"I'm afraid there's been a bit of a problem," said their uncle's voice. He sounded worried. "I'm afraid the Kenya Wildlife Service may not get to the waterhole in time."

"Then it's up to us?" Ben asked.

"Don't try any heroics," their uncle warned. "Just try to get some footage of the hunters on your BUGs that we can pass off as a tourist video. Over and out." The communicator clicked off.

Zoe turned to Ben. "We still have to try to stop them!" she said. Suddenly, a deafening shot rang out. "The hunters!"

Ben and Zoe raced along the elephant path toward the sound.

When they passed a baobab tree, they drew back in horror at the terrible scene.

A full-grown elephant cow lay on her side. Blood was seeping from a wound in her flank, forming a dark red pool under her belly. She wasn't moving. Her young calf stood over her, desperately trying to lift her back up with his little trunk. The children could see he had a wire wrapped around his back leg and the wound was oozing yellow pus. The calf looked almost too weak to stand.

"It's Tomboi!" cried Zoe. "We have to stop the hunters from killing him!"

Zoe leaped forward, but Ben quickly pulled her back. "Stay back!" he whispered. "The hunters will see us."

The little calf's cries made Zoe begin to sob. "We can't just sit and watch!" she said.

"We have to wait," Ben said firmly. "It's too dangerous."

The sound of angry yelling reached them from somewhere nearby. It was Mr. Hall's voice. "You idiot, Lester!" he said. "What were you thinking, grabbing my arm like that! You messed up my aim."

"Don't worry, Mr. Hall," Chitundu said quickly. "It was still a really good shot. I'm sure you killed her. I'll check."

"You shouldn't have done it, Dad!" Lester yelled. "It's cruel!"

"Don't be silly, boy," Mr. Hall said. "This is for sport. And now it's your turn. Here's your gun. Hold it like Chitundu showed you." He pointed at Tomboi. "The calf's a sitting duck, so take your shot. And don't let me down!"

"I told you, Dad, I won't do it!" Lester was almost crying. "You can't make me."

"Good for Lester!" Ben muttered through his teeth.

"Look, Ben," said Zoe, peering round the tree trunk. "The mother's chest is still moving!" She squeezed her brother's arm and smiled. "She's alive! Maybe we weren't too late! As soon as the hunters leave we can go and —"

Ben pointed as Chitundu walked toward Tomboi's mother, his rifle slung over his shoulder.

Ben put his hand on Zoe's. "Chitundu's going to finish the job," he said. "Mr. Hall wants his trophy."

"Then we have to do something!" Zoe said.

"We wait for our chance, Zoe," Ben said. "I know it's hard, but Chitundu won't want any witnesses. He'd shoot us if we're seen."

Ben beckoned to his sister and they peered around the tree. Now they could see the father and son. To their amazement, Frank Hall was trying to wrestle the gun away from Lester with a look of fury on his face. His battered hat had fallen to the ground.

Zoe whipped out her BUG and held it up, filming the whole scene. She swung it around until Chitundu came into view next to the fallen elephant. "Now we have evidence," she said grimly.

"The thing's practically dead already with that bad leg," said Mr. Hall. "If you're not man enough to shoot it, then I will."

"Don't you dare," shouted Lester. "I won't let you!" He was struggling with his father like his life depended on it.

Ben turned to watch Chitundu. The hunter was crouching next to the mother elephant. Suddenly, Tomboi bellowed in panic and began to headbutt Chitundu. Chitundu just pushed him away with the butt of his gun.

"I was right," said Ben, watching the man. "He's going to finish her off."

"What can we do?" Zoe asked.

"We could get the other elephants to come," Ben said. "If they knew these two were in trouble, they'd be on their way."

"But they're probably too far off to hear," said Zoe.

"Not if I amplify Tomboi's call," said Ben. He held up his BUG and pressed record as Tomboi let out another desperate bellow. The little calf lay by his mother's side. With a huge effort, the mom raised her trunk and lovingly touched Tomboi's face. Then she lay completely still.

"Is it too late?" gulped Zoe.

"Not for Tomboi," said Ben. He turned up the BUG volume and played it back.

The sound blasted into the air. Chitundu whipped around, trying to determine where it was coming from.

"That's too close to be an elephant," he said to himself. He began to walk toward Zoe and Ben's hiding place.

Ben and Zoe slithered backward, desperate to stay hidden. Using the barrel of his gun, Chitundu pushed the leaves and branches aside. He was coming closer. If Zoe or Ben broke cover, they knew he'd see them. If they stayed where they were, he'd find them for sure. They were trapped.

"Is there someone there?" asked Chitundu, raising his gun to his shoulder.

Ben and Zoe froze. Suddenly, a deafening gunshot rang out, followed by an angry curse. Chitundu hurried back through the undergrowth. The children followed quietly. They saw Lester, white with shock, holding his gun limply in one hand.

"You shot me!" Mr. Hall cried.

"It — it was an accident!" Lester cried. "I'm so sorry!"

"That's terrible," Zoe said. "Even Mr. Hall doesn't deserve to get shot."

"Agreed," Ben said. "But Lester did us a favor — they'll have to go back to the lodge now. The minute they're gone, we'll be able to help Tomboi."

Chitundu took the gun from Lester and laid it on the ground. He kneeled next to his client. "Where is the wound?" he asked urgently.

"My foot!" Mr. Hall croaked. "My own son shot me."

"I didn't mean to, Dad," Lester said shakily.

Mr. Hall yelped as Chitundu removed
his boot and sock. "It is not serious,"
Chitundu said. "The bullet just grazed your
big toe. It's hardly bleeding. I will dress it."

Lester sighed. "I don't know why you're
so relieved," Mr. Hall said, wincing as
Chitundu cleaned his wound. "You've
ruined the whole hunt. Give me the gun.
I'll shoot the calf."

Ben and Zoe stared at each other. The
nightmare wasn't over after all.

But suddenly Chitundu looked up. He was listening intently to distant sounds from along the track. "We can't risk staying any longer," he said. "The rest of the herd is coming."

"Yes!" said Zoe. "Your plan worked, Ben."

"Even though we almost got shot in the process," Ben added gravely.

Mr. Hall staggered to his feet. "I can't walk all the way back," he said angrily. "You'll have to call a jeep."

"There's no time," Chitundu said. "It's too dangerous to wait here." He took Mr. Hall firmly by the arm and helped him limp away.

The minute the hunters were gone, Ben and Zoe crawled out of their hiding place and approached the two elephants.

Ben and Zoe took off their backpacks and kneeled by the elephants. "We have to act quickly!" said Zoe.

Ben inspected the calf's injured leg. "This is horrible," he said. "There's so much swelling I can hardly see the snare." He made a gagging sound. "And the infection stinks!"

As gently as he could, he tried to untie the wire, but Tomboi stiffened and gave a bellow of pain.

Zoe stroked Tomboi's wrinkled head. "Stay calm," she said. "We want to help."

"We need sedation," said Ben.

Zoe snapped into action. She pulled the tranquilizing gun from her backpack. Ben stood up and aimed it into Tomboi's leg. Soon, the little bull calf was unconscious.

There was a harsh cry above them. They
looked up to see huge birds circling around
them.

"Vultures!" cried Zoe. She stood up and
waved her arms angrily at them.

"The antibiotic in the solution is very
strong so it should get to work soon," said
Ben, as he tried to loosen the snare with a
pair of pliers.

A loud trumpeting from along the track made the children leap to their feet. Through the trees they could see the herd of elephants approaching, the huge matriarch at the front.

"You hide, Zoe," said Ben. "I'll join you in a minute. I've almost got this wire free." His teeth were clenched and sweat was trickling down his face.

"We're in this together," Zoe said. "I'll help." She raised Tomboi's limp foot. "Try the other side."

Ben eased the point of his pliers under the wire. "Got it!" he said. There was a click and the snare sprang free from the little elephant's foot.

Zoe quickly threw their equipment into her backpack.

"He'll be back on his feet in a few minutes," Ben said, retrieving the dart that had sedated Tomboi. "Erika told me it only lasts a few minutes."

"Look!" Zoe said urgently.

Ben glanced up. The huge matriarch was a few yards away. Her eyes were wild with fear as she called anxiously to the two fallen members of her herd.

Ben and Zoe backed away to the safety of the trees as the herd surrounded Tomboi and his mother.

Some pressed forward, feeling the cow all over with their trunks. Others paced around the group, roaring their trumpeting call. Ben and Zoe could just see the matriarch curling her long trunk around Tomboi, who was struggling to get to his feet.

With the help of two other cows, the matriarch lifted him up and supported him gently, holding him against her leg.

"Uh-oh!" said Zoe. "I think they see us."

One of the largest elephants of the group was making its way toward them. Ben and Zoe cowered in fear as the huge gray beast towered above their hiding place. Then it raised its trunk, grasped the branch over their heads, and tore it away.

Others began to tear branches from the surrounding trees.

They laid them gently over the lifeless body of Tomboi's mother.

"It looks like a sort of funeral," Ben whispered in awe. "She must be dead."

Zoe watched, tears falling silently from her cheeks.

The elephants stood silently around the mound of leaves. The matriarch was the first to move. She gently steered Tomboi away with her trunk. The little elephant gave one last pitiful look back. Then he limped away with the herd.

Ben took out his BUG and pressed the WILD call key.

"I've managed to get an update from the Kenya Wildlife Service," said Uncle Stephen's voice. "They should be on their way soon."

"They're too late to save Tomboi's mother," said Ben. "She's been shot."

"And Tomboi?" their uncle's voice asked.

Ben told him everything that had happened. "The hunters are walking back to the lodge now," he finished.

"Well, they won't get far," Dr. Fisher said sternly. "I'll tip off the KWS so they can pick them up. I'll also make sure they get Zoe's video evidence. That way, they'll have a strong case against Mr. Hall and Chitundu."

Her eyes full of tears, Zoe walked over to say goodbye to Tomboi's mother. She bent down and stroked the elephant's forehead.

Then she jumped up. Frantically, she swept away the burial coverings and put her hand on the elephant's side. She was silent for a moment, but then jumped to her feet. "Ben!" she yelled. "Call Uncle Stephen back — Tomboi's mother is still alive!"

CHAPTER 11

SAFE AND SOUND

Two days later, a small group of hikers stood by the waterhole. It was a chilly morning and tops of the trees were lit with dawn's golden glow.

Wambua turned to the tourists in his party. "Stand very still," he said, a big smile on his face. "Here come our beloved elephants."

Ben, Zoe, and Erika watched eagerly as the pale-skinned matriarch led her herd down to the water on the opposite bank.

Lester Hall stood slightly apart, snapping photos of the scene.

"See the little calf?" Wambua asked. "Tomboi has just had a very lucky escape from hunters, thanks to the Kenya Wildlife Service."

Ben and Zoe grinned at each other. No one could ever know WILD's part in the rescue, of course.

"Wambua sounds happy," said Ben, as the old man walked off. "No one will stop them from protecting the elephants now."

"Tomboi's leg is healing nicely," Zoe whispered to her brother, as they watched the little elephant wading through some thick reeds. "I wish we could tell him his mother's alive and being healed."

"And that those hunters won't be bothering them again," Ben added.

Mr. Hall and Chitundu had been whisked away to the police station, each blaming the other, until they'd seen a video from an anonymous source — Zoe's footage. After they saw that, both Chitundu and Mr. Hall confessed everything.

The village was relieved. Runo brought Zoe and Ben to Wambua so they could all visit the elephants.

"I'm glad Lester's mom can't get out here for a few more days," said Ben. "He's cool — nothing like his dad."

"It'll be good to have him with us for the rest of our stay," Zoe said.

Just then, Lester Hall came over to join them. He held out his camera to show his photos. "This is what I came to Africa for," he said, showing them his photos.

"They look great," Zoe said. "You'll have tons to show your mom."

Lester looked serious for a moment. "Thanks for letting me hang out with you after what happened," he said quietly.

"It's okay," said Ben. "See how healthy the calf looks? You're a hero. I mean, that's what I heard, anyway. That you wouldn't let your dad shoot him," he added quickly.

Lester blushed. "Thanks," he said shyly.

Tomboi suddenly broke into a trot, sucked up a trunkful of water, and blasted the matriarch. She splashed Tomboi back, and he rolled over in the mud.

"That's one happy little elephant!" Zoe said, laughing.

THE AUTHORS

Jan Burchett and **Sara Vogler** were already friends when they discovered they both wanted to write children's books, and that it was much more fun to do it together. They have since written over a hundred and thirty stories ranging from educational books and stories for younger readers to young adult fiction. They have written for series such as Dinosaur Cove and Beast Quest, and they are authors of the Gargoylz books.

THE ILLUSTRATOR

Diane Le Feyer discovered a passion for drawing and animation at the age of five. In 2002, she graduated with honors from the Ecole Emile Cohl school of design. Diane worked as a character designer, 3D modeler, and animator in the video games industry before joining the Cartoon Saloon animation studio, where she worked as a director, animator, illustrator, and character designer. Diane was also a part of the early design and development of the movie *The Secret of Kells*.

GLOSSARY

antibiotic (an-ti-bye-OT-ik)—a drug that kills bacteria and is used to cure infections and diseases

carcass (KAR-kuhss)—the body of a dead animal

expedition (ek-spuh-DISH-uhn)—a long journey for a special purpose, such as exploring or hunting

matriarch (MAY-tree-ark)—the female head of a family or tribe of animals

poach (POHCH)—to catch fish or animals illegally on someone else's land

recruited (ri-KROOT-id)—got a person to join

sedation (si-DAY-shuhn)—a state of calm or sleepiness caused by a drug like a tranquilizer

shimmering (SHIM-ur-ing)—shining with a faint, unsteady light

taxidermy TAK-suh-dur-mee)—the practice of preparing and preserving the skins of animals and of stuffing and mounting them in lifelike form

urgent (UR-juhnt)—if something is urgent, it needs very quick or immediate attention

velocity (vuh-LOSS-uh-tee)—speed

AFRICAN ELEPHANT
STATUS: VULNERABLE

The African elephant is the largest living land animal. They are found in East, South, and West Africa in deserts and forests. They have the biggest ears of any animal, are very smart, and can weigh up to the equivalent of five cars. Despite their impressive size and intelligence, African elephants face many threats to their survival.

LOSS OF HABITAT: The biggest threat to the African elephant is the loss of their habitat. Elephant land is being broken up or reduced by village expansion and crop growing.

HUMAN CONTACT: The introduction of farms to elephant habitats also causes elephants to come into contact with humans. Elephants will travel to farms to eat crops, causing humans to fight back — sometimes with deadly force.

POACHING: Even though it is now illegal to trade in ivory, hunters are still killing elephants for their tusks and selling the ivory in illegal or underground markets. Sadly, the demand for ivory is still very high in some areas, making poaching more profitable for illegal hunters.

BUT IT'S NOT ALL BAD FOR THE AFRICAN ELEPHANT! Several wildlife foundations are trying to help elephants in Africa. In Kenya, they're working to stop the conflicts between elephants and people by developing ways to prevent elephants from eating crops. Special fencing warns rangers when an elephant tries to break through it.